Upsy Daisy loves the Ninky Nonk!

Andrew Davenport

Once upon a time in the Night Garden...

Upsy Daisy came to play.

Upsy Daisy,
Here I come,
I'm the only Upsy one!
I'm the only Daisy too,
Ipsy Upsy Daisy doo!

One day, Upsy Daisy decided to kiss
everything in the garden.
What a funny idea, Upsy Daisy!

Upsy Daisy doo!

First of all she kissed
her friend, Igglepiggle.

Then Upsy Daisy kissed a tree,

Upsy Daisy doo!

a flower,

Upsy Daisy doo!

the Magical Gazebo,

and another tree.

What a lot of things
there are to kiss
in the garden,
Upsy Daisy.

Ting-ting!

Upsy Daisy decided to go by Ninky Nonk.

What a very clever way to kiss everything in the garden, Upsy Daisy.

Ting-ting!

The Ninky Nonk stopped.
Look at that.
What a lot of daisies!

Upsy Daisy doo!

Upsy Daisy gave every single daisy
a big Upsy Daisy kiss.

Ting-ting!

The Ninky Nonk stopped again.
Who's here?

Makka Pakka!

Hello Makka Pakka.

Upsy Daisy doo!

Upsy Daisy gave Makka Pakka
a big Upsy Daisy kiss.
Makka Pakka was very pleased.

Oh dear.
What a funny noise!

What was the matter
with the Ninky Nonk?
Do you know?

Has Upsy Daisy
remembered to give
the Ninky Nonk a kiss?

Upsy Daisy!

Upsy Daisy gave the Ninky Nonk
a great big Upsy Daisy kiss.

Upsy Daisy doo!

Ting-ting!

What a happy
Ninky Nonk.

Upsy Daisy!

The Ninky Nonk
wanted a kiss.

Isn't that a pip?

Once upon a time
in the Night Garden,

Upsy Daisy kissed a tree,
Igglepiggle, all the daisies
and Makka Pakka.

Upsy Daisy, you forgot
to kiss the Ninky Nonk!

Upsy Daisy doo!

What a happy Ninky Nonk.

Thank you,
Upsy Daisy.

Time to go to sleep everybody.

Go to sleep, Upsy Daisy.

Go to sleep, Makka Pakka.

Go to sleep, Pontipines.

Go to sleep, Tombliboos.

Go to sleep, Haahoos.

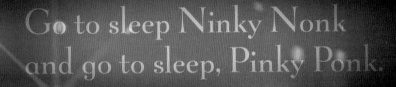

Go to sleep Ninky Nonk
and go to sleep, Pinky Ponk.

Wait a minute.
Somebody is not in bed!
Who's not in bed?
Igglepiggle is not in bed!

Don't worry, Igglepiggle...
it's time to go.